Effie the Outrageous Elf

Little Horrors

Effie the Outrageous Elf

Tiffany Mandrake

Illustrated by Martin Chatterton

LITTLE HARE
www.littleharebooks.com

Little Hare Books
an imprint of
Hardie Grant Egmont
85 High Street
Prahran, Victoria 3181, Melbourne

www.littleharebooks.com

First published in 2010

National Library of Australia
Cataloguing-in-Publication entry

Mandrake, Tiffany.

Effie the outrageous elf / Tiffany Mandrake;
illustrator, Martin Chatterton.

978 1 921541 87 2 (pbk.)

Mandrake, Tiffany. Little horrors; 5.

For primary school age.

Elves—Juvenile fiction.

Chatterton, Martin.

A823.3

Cover design by Martin Chatterton
Set in 16/22 pt Bembo by Clinton Ellicott
Printed by Griffin Press
Printed in Adelaide, Australia, July 2010

5 4 3 2 1

This product conforms to CPSIA 2008

Contents

A Note from Tiffany Mandrake

Psst, this is me, Tiffany Mandrake, speaking to you from my cosy, creepy cottage in the grounds of Hags' Abademy of Badness. The Abademy is a place where bad fairies go to study how to be truly bad. It's not far from where you live, but you probably won't see it. The fairy-breed use special spells to make sure you don't. It is run by three water hags, Maggie Nabbie, Auld Anni and Kirsty Breeks.

The hags started the Abademy because too many fairies were doing sweet deeds.

Sweet deeds are not always good deeds, and the world needs a bit of honest badness for balance. Otherwise, we humans get slack and lazy. The Abademy provides that balance. To enter the Abademy, young fairies must earn a Badge of Badness.

This is the story of Effie Redwood, an outrageous elf who loved applause and attention.

I don't come into this story at all, but the polly-fae told me about what Effie did at the Big Top Circus. I promised not to tell anyone . . . but you can keep a secret, can't you?

Sure you can.

So listen . . . And remember, not a word to anyone!

1. Effie Redwood

'Look at me!' Effie Redwood called, as she bounced on a branch in her bright red boots. 'Wheeeeeee!' she yelled, as she sprang into the air. She landed on the forest floor, where her brother, Om, sat with the other elves. Their legs were crossed and their palms faced upwards.

'I looped the loop twice that time! Did you see?' Effie asked Om.

'No,' said Om. 'I'm thinking deep thoughts. *The oak is the child of the acorn. The acorn is the child of the oak.*'

Effie sighed. Om and the others were always thinking. They hardly ever did anything else.

'I can think deep thoughts, too,' she said. 'Watch me, Om!' She sprang back into the tree. Her hair swung behind her and her red cape flapped under her wings. She perched cross-legged on a branch, and turned up her palms, just like Om.

'*The tree grows in the ground,*' she shouted. '*An elf sits in a tree. The elf flies through the air and loops the loop three times!* Watch me, Om!' She dived forward and tumbled head over heels. '*Wheeeeeee!*'

She flung out her arms as she landed. 'Tah-*dah*! Aren't I clever, Om?' she said.

'*Wind blows and blows. Oak grows and knows,*' said Om.

'Did you like my trick?'

'No,' said Om. He scowled at Effie. 'You're outrageous. Besides, you never bother to get the words right.'

'But I thought deep thoughts about an elf flying from a tree.'

'Elves can think deep thoughts only when they are sitting still and being quiet,' said Om. 'You were showing off. Go away and leave us in peace.'

'But, *Om* . . .' said Effie.

'*Wind must roam. It knows no home,*' said the other elves.

Effie's chin wobbled. She tried so hard to fit in, but the elves always ignored her. They didn't like her tricks.

'I'll do what I like,' Effie said. 'So there!'

The elves closed their eyes.

Effie flew back into the tree. She gathered a pocketful of acorns and dropped one on Om's head. Om shuffled along on his bottom to get out of range, but he didn't open his eyes.

Effie was about to do a wind spell to make the acorns fly farther when she heard a faint sound in the distance. She forgot her anger and climbed to the top of the oak tree to spy on the human road that passed by the forest.

She was used to seeing cars, but today a line of red, gold and green vans and trucks was rolling down the road. The first van bore the words: BIG TOP CIRCUS. The trucks had pictures of humans in red and gold, doing tricks. And in the back of one of the open trucks, Effie spotted two human women in sparkly outfits doing handstands together and laughing.

Effie sniffed a strange smell of sawdust, horses, hay and paint. 'Look!' she cried. 'Look, Om! Here comes a travelling show!'

At first, Om ignored her, but as the parade of vehicles came closer, he twitched and frowned. He opened his eyes and glanced at the other elves.

'It's a circus! Outrageous!' they all said together.

'It's wonderful!' cried Effie, kicking her boots against a branch in excitement. 'Come up and see the circus, Om!'

'Don't be stupid,' said Om. 'Why would we want to see noisy horrible humans?'

'Oh, *please*, Om!' begged Effie. 'These humans aren't horrible. They're fun! Come up here and look before they go! For me?'

'No,' said Om. 'If you think humans are so much fun, why don't you stop bothering us and go and join them?'

'I will then!' said Effie. She sprang

from the tree and landed in front of her brother. 'Om?'

'Go on,' said Om. 'It will be more peaceful without you here anyway.'

Tears welled up in Effie's eyes. She gave a big sniffle, and leapt into the air. She could hardly see for tears, but she soon caught up with the rumble of vehicles. She flew as fast as she could, until she caught hold of the luggage rack on top of the last van.

'I know I'll fit in with these circus folk!' Effie said to herself.

Her cloak streamed behind her as she flipped onto the roof.

'Tah-*dah*!' she yelled, tossing her long hair out of her eyes and swinging over in a backflip.

'Yay! Nice one, Effie!' squawked a voice in her ear.

2. Effie Gets an Invitation

Effie jumped as two sets of claws dug into her shoulder.

'*Waaaarrrrk!*' yelled the voice. 'You nearly sent me flying! Is that any way to treat your new best friend?'

'Huh?' Effie grabbed the thing from her shoulder and stared at it. 'You're a parrot!' she said.

The thing had red glowing eyes, a

hooked beak and scarlet feathers. 'I am *not* a parrot,' it said.

'What are you, then?' asked Effie.

'I am the polly-fae,' said the creature. 'I'm a kind of imp, a fairy fetch, and there is only one of me in the whole world.' It flipped its wings and bowed. 'I have bird DNA.'

'Your feathers are red,' said Effie. 'I love red. You match my favourite boots and my cape. Do you like seeing tricks? The elves don't.'

'I cheered, didn't I?' the polly-fae said. It clapped its wings and yelled, 'Hurrah for Effie Redwood!' Then it drew one gold claw up to its chest and cocked its head. 'What's a forest elf doing on a circus van?' it asked.

'I want to join the circus,' said Effie. 'I don't fit in with the elves.'

The polly-fae shrugged its wings.
'Of course you don't fit in with the elves,
Effie. You're a bad fairy.'

'No, I'm not,' Effie said.

The polly-fae squawked with laughter.
'Sure you are. You're an outrageous
show-off! So it's just as well I have *this*!'
It plucked a feather from its tail.
'*Shazammmm!*' it said, poking the feather
at Effie. 'This is your invitation to apply
for a Badge of Badness!'

'What's that?' Effie asked. She settled
cross-legged on top of the van.

The fetch perched on her left knee.
'A Badge of Badness is a special prize
that's given to young fairies who are good
at being bad,' it said. 'If you win one, you
can go to Hags' Abademy of Badness.'

'What's an Abademy of Badness?'
asked Effie.

'It's a special school for bad fairies,' said
the polly-fae. 'It's run by three water
hags, Maggie Nabbie, Kirsty Breeks and
Auld Anni. They think you'd fit in there.
They passed through your forest last week
and saw you annoying all the elves. I'm
here to help you win your Badge of
Badness.'

'And I can win one by showing off?'
said Effie.

'We *love* show-offs at the Abademy,' said the polly-fae, 'but you have to do something special to win a Badge of Badness.' It offered Effie the invitation again, and she took it.

Effie watched as words appeared on the feather's surface. '*Are you an* **outrageous elf***?*' she read. '*Do you relish* **showing off, and do you yearn for applause***? Answer Yes or No.*'

'Well?' said the polly-fae.

Effie thought about it. 'Yes!' she said. She read on. '*You are invited to apply for a Badge of Badness from the Hags' Abademy. To qualify, you must create and perform a new and original act of breathtaking badness. Answer I Will or I Won't.*'

'Hmm,' said Effie. 'Actually, I Won't. Sorry.'

'What?' squawked the polly-fae.

Effie shook her head. 'This Abademy sounds interesting, but I don't need to go there. I belong with the circus. These people are noisy and silly, and they like doing tricks. I'll fit right in here.'

'They're *humans*,' said the polly-fae. 'They're not fairy-breed like you.'

'I don't care what they are, as long as they like me for who I am,' said Effie.

3. Circus Daze

Effie practised backflips on top of the van,
then spun around on the tips of her toes.

'Yay!' yelled the polly-fae, and clapped
its wings. 'Brilliant!'

'You're still here!' said Effie in surprise.

'Why wouldn't I be?' said the fae.

'I told you I didn't want to go to the
Abademy.'

'Friends stick together,' said the fetch.

'If you won't come with me, I'll come with you.'

Effie was puzzled. 'Aren't you cross?'

The fetch scratched its ear. 'No, it's up to you,' it said. 'The hags will be disappointed, though. They were looking forward to you joining them.'

The van slowed down. 'Looks like we've arrived,' the polly-fae said, and flew onto Effie's shoulder.

Effie peered at a sign beside the road. *'The Town of Appleboffin Welcomes the Big Top Circus!'* she read.

The vans and trucks turned off the road and parked in a large grassy space backed by trees. The circus people got out and unloaded the vehicles. Effie perched on the tallest truck and watched as humans and horses gathered around an enormous canvas tent.

'That tent is called the big top,' said the polly-fae. 'The circus acts perform in a ring inside, and people pay money to see them. Look, those horses are helping to put it up.'

Effie stared as the tent rose like a huge green bubble.

'Heave!' yelled a plump woman in long red boots. 'Heave!'

'We *are* heaving, Marigold!' muttered a girl with fluffy blonde hair and several bead necklaces. 'I'm a star. This circus would be nothing without me and Hoopla.' She gestured to a small pony that was tethered outside a nearby tent. 'I shouldn't have to haul on ropes!' the girl added.

'I'm a bigger star than you, Blanche,' a little girl in tights said to the blonde girl. Then she turned to the woman in the red boots and said, 'I'm tired, Auntie Marigold.'

'I know you are, Vesta dearie!' the woman replied. 'But we must all work together.'

'Marigold looks nice,' said Effie. She hugged herself. 'I'm going to fit right in here!'

The big top settled into place, and the humans fastened their ropes to large iron pegs stuck into the ground. Effie flew to bounce on top of the tent.

'*Wheeeee!*' she called. Her feet shot out from underneath her and she slid down the bouncy canvas. When she hit the ground, she leapt into the air in a somersault. 'Tah-*dah*!' she said.

'Way to go, Effie Redwood!' squawked the polly-fae, clapping its wings.

Effie flew up to do it again. Then she went to see what the circus folk were doing. She found them carrying boxes of costumes into a small dressing tent.

'OK, everyone!' yelled Marigold. 'It's teatime! Let's make some sandwiches.'

'It's not my job,' said Blanche.

'I have to rest before the show,' said Vesta. 'Dodley can do it.'

A plump young man in floppy green trousers scowled. 'Why should I? I have to rest, too,' he said.

'I'm hungry,' whined Vesta.

'I'll see to it,' said Marigold. She went off into one of the vans. The others kept bickering and complaining until Marigold came back with sandwiches, nuts and fruit. 'Tuck in!' she said, smiling. 'This will make us all feel better.'

'Yum!' Effie said. She snatched an apple and a fistful of cheese sandwiches.

The polly-fae seized a walnut and cracked the shell. 'It's a good job we're wearing DNM spells, so nobody will spot us stealing this food,' it said.*

---

*DNM, or Don't Notice Me, spells are special spells the fairy-breed use to stop humans noticing them. A bad fairy wearing a DNM spell can get up to all kinds of mischief.

Effie watched as the humans ate their meal and then scrambled into their brightly coloured performance clothes.

'A very important man, called Mr Pop Topper, is coming to watch the show tonight,' Marigold said.

Vesta put on a spangled cape. 'I must look my very best when I perform my fly-and-flip for him,' she said.

'Bother,' said Blanche. 'I haven't groomed Hoopla yet, but he must look spotless for Pop Topper. Dodley, you do it. You've finished your make-up.'

'Why should I?' said Dodley. 'Get Zena to groom him.'

'Zena——' Blanche said.

A dark-haired girl in an orange leotard shook her head. 'Do it yourself, Blanche,' she said. 'I have to sew sequins on my outfit so Pop Topper notices me.'

Effie spat apple pips into Dodley's make-up pot as she watched the circus folk arguing with each other. 'I wonder who this Pop Topper person is?' she said.

Just then, a group of humans carrying musical instruments hurried past them and into the big top. Shortly after this, Effie heard music coming from inside the tent.

The polly-fae cocked its head. 'The audience is arriving,' it said.

'*Oooh!*' Effie squealed. 'It's show time!'

She and the polly-fae flew into the big top to watch the show.

4. Vesta Fiesta

The big top's floor was covered in
sawdust, and a huge safety net hung above
it. Above the net was a high wire with a
platform at each end, and a trapeze.

'There you are!' said Effie, as the polly-
fae swooped to perch on her shoulder.
'Look at all these people!'

'They're here to watch the acts,' said
the polly-fae.

'*Oooh!*' Effie jigged about with excitement.

Marigold strode into the circus ring. She was dressed in a sparkly jacket and her bright red boots. She carried a huge black whip in her hand.

'Ladies and gentlemen!' she roared. 'Welcome to the Big Top Circus!'

Crack! She snapped her whip in the air. 'A special welcome to our guest, Mr Pop Topper, of Topper's Treats—the nation's favourite sweet shop!'

A man in a tall hat waved from a seat in the front row of the audience.

'*Yayyyyy!*' yelled the crowd.

'Here's Ballerina Blanche Babiole with her perfect pony, *Hoopla*!' cried Marigold.

Crack! went the whip, and Blanche ran into the ring. Her pony trotted after her.

Crack!

Blanche sprang onto the pony's back.

Crack!

The crowd clapped as Blanche balanced on Hoopla's rump and cantered around the ring.

Crack!

'Introducing Dodley the *Colourful Clown*!' cried Marigold. The crowd clapped again as Dodley rushed in, juggling six eggs and a hoop.

'*Oooh!*' said Effie, as Dodley jumped onto a small trampoline and went on juggling. '*I* can do everything Dodley and Blanche have done so far, only better. All these people will be applauding *me* once I join the circus!'

Crack!

Vesta entered in her sparkly cape.

'Please welcome high-wire artiste

Tiny Vesta Fiesta!' yelled Marigold. 'Vesta is the youngest person ever to perform the death–defying *fly-and-flip*!'

Vesta ran to a rope ladder that dangled from the ceiling.

'She's going to walk along that wire,' said the polly-fae.

'*Oooooh!*' roared the crowd as Vesta climbed the ladder.

Effie hugged herself. '*I* can do that, too! It's easy-peasy.'

Vesta's cape swirled as she reached the high wire and stepped onto it. Then she walked carefully along the wire with her arms outstretched.

'Vesta Fiesta! Vesta Fiesta!' the crowd roared.

Vesta wobbled a little and the crowd gasped. She continued along the wire, and the humans applauded again.

Effie was too excited to sit still.

'I'm going to take off my DNM spell, so the humans can see me,' she told the polly-fae. 'Then I'll run onto that wire and be the star of the show.'

'Go on then,' said the fetch.

Effie hesitated. 'I just have to say the magic words Om taught me to take off my DNM spell.' She frowned. 'Um, *Earth, wind,* er ... *sky, sea ... Get ready to see me!*' she said. 'That should do it!'

The polly-fae clapped its wings and flew up to perch on one of the posts that held up the high wire. 'Way to go, Effie Redwood!' it yelled.

Effie flew up and looped the loop under the roof of the big top.

Vesta reached the end of the wire and sprang to the trapeze. She swung back and forth, then flipped over to hang by her legs. Then, she turned a somersault.

The crowd cheered, and Effie looped the loop again, tumbling over and over in the air, with the applause echoing in her ears. She had never been so happy.

'These people *love* my tricks!' cried Effie, landing in the sawdust. 'I'm going on the trapeze right now!'

5. Effie Misses Her Chance

Effie's wings fluttered under her cape as she swung herself up the ladder. She reached the platform and began dancing along the wire towards the trapeze. At the same time, Vesta Fiesta began her return trip. Just before they met in the middle of the wire, Vesta began to turn a somersault. Normally she found this easy, but tonight Effie was in the way.

'*Aghhhhh!*' yelled Vesta as she crashed into Effie.

'Watch it!' said Effie, using her wings to keep her balance.

Vesta didn't have wings. She tumbled from the high wire with her cape flapping around her.

The crowd screamed in terror as Vesta landed in the safety net, bounced, and lay still.

Marigold cracked her whip. 'Keep calm, everyone,' she called. She strode to the net. 'Are you all right, dearie?' she said to Vesta. 'You aren't usually careless enough to slip.'

'I'm not careless!' snapped Vesta. 'It wasn't my fault. Someone got in my way.'

Marigold laughed. 'Don't be silly, Vesta. There was no one there. Get back up on that wire and do your fly-and-flip.'

Vesta glared at her. 'I won't!' she said,
and ran from the ring.

The audience murmured. Effie wanted
them to cheer for her again, so she raised
her arms and pranced out along the wire,
moving twice as fast as Vesta had. She
fluttered her wings and twirled, spinning
like a top. Then she bowed.

The audience wriggled and rattled junk food packets.

'Tah-*dah*!' yelled Effie. She twirled again, but still the audience ignored her.

Effie turned to the polly-fae. 'Pol, what's wrong with them? Why don't they like my act any more?'

The polly-fae swooped down to her shoulder. 'The humans don't like your act because they *can't see you*!'

'But I took off my DNM spell!' said Effie.

'You got the words wrong,' said the fetch.

'But ...' Effie thought back. 'Maybe I should have said *Earth, wind, sky, TREES ... Get ready to see me*,' she admitted. 'Om says I'm careless with spells.' She sighed. 'But they cheered for me before ...'

'They were cheering Vesta Fiesta,' said the fetch. 'Never mind. I expect you enjoyed doing those tricks anyway.'

'I suppose so,' said Effie, but showing off wasn't much fun if no one saw.

Crack! went Marigold's whip. 'Zesty Zena Prince and the Zeppanellis!' she announced, and the dark-haired girl in the leotard cartwheeled into the ring, followed by several other tumblers.

'It's still my turn!' said Effie. 'Wait for me to take off my DNM spell!'

But she had missed her chance. The audience was watching Zena.

6. 'I'm Effie Redwood'

Effie sat in the safety net for the rest of the show. She hardly noticed the last few acts, because she was so disappointed.

'I *have* to join this circus properly,' she said to the polly-fae.

When the show was over, and the big top was empty, Effie carefully recited the magic words to remove her DNM spell and bounced out of the safety net.

She landed in the sawdust, and went looking for the performers.

She found them sharing a jug of lemonade on the grass in front of their dressing tent.

'Hello!' Effie said, smiling.

Marigold jumped. 'Where did you spring from?' she asked Effie.

'I'm going to join your circus,' said Effie.

Marigold sighed. 'Well, dearie, you've gone to a lot of trouble with your costume, but——'

'We don't want anyone else,' said Vesta.

'I'll show you my amazing act,' Effie said. 'I'm better than all of you, so of *course* you'll want me.'

'Don't be outrageous,' said Zena. 'Outsiders aren't allowed. Go away.'

Effie giggled. 'I'm not an outsider. I'm one of you! Watch me!' She threw herself into a handstand.

Blanche yawned. 'I'm tired of outsiders who think they're something special. Get rid of her, Dodley.'

'Why me?' said the clown.

Marigold clapped her hands. 'Give the child a chance.'

'There's no time,' said Zena. 'Pop Topper is coming to supper tonight, remember?'

Effie remembered Pop Topper from the show. 'Ooh, good,' she said, flipping upright again. 'I can show him my act!'

'I'm afraid Zena's right, dearie,' said Marigold. 'We're busy tonight, so run along back to your parents.'

'But you haven't watched my act. I can do lots of things!' said Effie.

Marigold smiled regretfully and turned her back on Effie. 'Go and get ready for Pop Topper,' she said to the others.

Grumbling, the circus folk went to change out of their costumes.

Effie followed them into the dressing tent. 'Watch me!' she said to Dodley as he removed his make-up. She stole a dozen eggs from a crate in the corner and began to juggle with them.

'*Wheeeee!* Look at me!' she said. The eggs spun through the air.

Dodley looked up. 'Stop that,' he snarled. 'You'll break them!'

Effie went on to Zena, who was brushing her hair at a mirror. 'I can do cartwheels, too,' she said.

'Go home,' said Zena.

'I *am* home,' said Effie. 'I'm part of the circus.'

'No, you're not,' said Zena.

Effie did a triple backflip right over Zena's head. 'Tah-*dah*!'

Zena peered at her own reflection. 'Go home!' she said again.

'But——' Effie began.

Marigold put her head in. 'Pop Topper is here,' she told the performers.

Zena, Vesta, Blanche and Dodley stopped what they were doing and hurried out of the tent.

Marigold was about to leave, too, when she spotted Effie. 'Go home, dearie,' she said and bustled away.

Of course, Effie followed her.

The polly-fae watched with interest. Effie was as stubborn as any bad fairy it had ever seen.

*

Marigold entered a small tent, closely followed by Effie and the polly-fae. The other acts were inside with the man in the tall hat who had been at the show.

'This is Pop Topper,' said Marigold. 'He's here to tell us how we could work with him and make lots of money. Over to you, Mr Topper!'

Pop Topper smiled. 'My shop, Topper's Treats, has invented a new type of bubblegum, and I want *you* to help me launch it,' he said.

Vesta Fiesta smiled. 'I adore bubblegum,' she said.

'I adore it even more,' said Blanche.

'I'm glad to hear it!' said Pop Topper. He went on, 'I call my gum *Big Pop Gum*. I want to advertise it like this.' He held up a banner that read:

Big Pop Gum makes you a Big Top Star!

Pop Topper spilt packets of gum onto
the table. The circus folk snatched for
them, and Effie bounced onto the table
and grabbed some, too.

'And what act do you do?' Pop Topper
asked Effie as she balanced on one toe.

'Everything!' said Effie. 'Look!' She
juggled with the packets.

Dodley grabbed at her, but Effie did a
backflip and landed gracefully on the
table, still juggling. 'Tah-*dah*!' she yelled.

'Do go home, dearie!' said Marigold. She turned to Pop Topper and said, 'She's not one of us.'

'She's just a show-off outsider,' said Vesta.

Dodley grabbed at Effie again, but missed. She zipped to the end of the table, her cape flying behind her.

'But who is she?' asked Pop Topper.

'I'm Effie Redwood!' said Effie, spinning on one toe. 'Tah-*dah*!' She flung out her arms, sending packets of gum flying, and bowed. 'Did you like my trick?'

She threw herself into a handstand, and backflipped all the way along the table. Then she bounced up again. 'Tah-*dah*!'

'She doesn't belong,' said Vesta.

'She keeps showing off,' said Zena.

'She's a silly outsider,' sneered Dodley.

Marigold held up her hand. 'There's no need to be unkind, people. But really, this child shouldn't be here while we're having a business supper.'

She gestured to Dodley and Blanche, and said, 'Take her out and see if you can find her parents.' Then she turned back to Pop Topper and sighed. 'Unfortunately, the circus draws a lot of fans who want to join us. Please don't encourage her.'

Effie dodged out of Dodley's and Blanche's reach. She felt like crying. Why wouldn't these people just give her a chance? She'd been so sure she'd belong with them. But it was no use. She sprang from the table, put her DNM spell back on, and flew out of the tent.

7. The Invitation Again

'It isn't fair!' stormed Effie as she landed on the roof of the big top, with the polly-fae beside her. 'I tried to show them what I could do, but they kept on calling me an outsider!' She hugged her knees and put her chin on her arms. 'Why are they so horrible to me, Pol? They ought to be pleased to have me in the circus.'

'Your tricks are better than theirs,' said the polly-fae. 'You make them look slow and silly. They don't like feeling like that.'

'It isn't fair,' muttered Effie, again. 'The elves didn't want me, and now these circus people don't want me either.' A tear ran down her cheek. 'I don't fit in anywhere, Pol.' She unwrapped some of the Big Pop Gum that she'd grabbed, and offered it to the fetch.

'You'd fit in just fine at Hags' Abademy of Badness,' said the polly-fae, taking some bubblegum. 'The hags would love to have you there.'

Effie wiped her eyes on her cape and bounced up. 'Then take me to the Abademy right now.'

'You can't just *go* to the Abademy. You have to prove you belong there by doing a big bad deed. It's all in your invitation, remember?' the polly-fae said. It plucked another feather from its tail, and Effie took it.

'Well?' said the polly-fae, lifting the piece of gum in its claw. 'Will you create and perform a new and original act of breathtaking badness, like the invitation says?'

'I Will!' said Effie. In her mind she heard a roar of applause. She looked down at the feather–invitation and read out the words that had appeared. *'The Hags' Abademy is a school where bad fairies learn to balance badness in the world. Go forth and be bad. The polly-fae will help you.'*

Effie wasn't quite sure how to do a bad deed.

'I annoyed the elves and the circus people by showing off,' she said to the fetch. 'Is that a bad deed?'

'Showing off is not a big bad deed,' said the polly-fae. Its voice sounded muffled. 'You have to prove you can *plan* a bad deed and then make it happen.' It scratched at its beak with one claw.

Effie thought about it. 'The circus people called me an outsider and wouldn't look at my act,' she said. 'What if I spoil *their* acts and get lots of applause for mine? Does that sound bad?'

The polly-fae said nothing. Its claw seemed to be stuck to its beak.

'What's wrong?' asked Effie.

''At 'um,' muttered the fetch. 'It's 'uck.'

Effie helped the polly-fae get the gum off its beak.

'Stopping the circus people from giving good performances, and then doing a great performance yourself sounds like a *very* bad deed,' the polly-fae said, when it could talk again.

Effie decided to tackle the first part first. She thought hard of ways to ruin the others' performances. 'The circus people love that bubblegum,' she said.

'Huh!' said the fetch. 'Nasty sticky stuff.'

'Exactly,' said Effie. 'We'll have fun with gum. Help me steal a good supply. I've just thought of a plan which means I'm sure to get my Badge of Badness and go to the Abademy. So there.'

8. Fun with Gum

Effie and the polly-fae sneaked into the tent where the circus people were having supper.

'That's settled, then,' Pop Topper was saying. 'Please chew gum at every show, and praise it to the audience. I'll have television cameras to record your acts.'

'Make sure the cameras focus on my fly-and-flip,' said Vesta.

'They'll love my bareback ballet act!' said Blanche.

'Where's the gum?' the polly-fae said to Effie. No one else heard because it was wearing its DNM spell.

Effie was wearing her DNM spell, too. She glanced at the table, but the packets of gum had disappeared. 'It must be in their pockets,' she said.

Effie sidled up behind Marigold and stuck her fingers into her pockets. Marigold glanced down and brushed at her trousers. Effie jumped away with two packets of gum between her fingers. Then, she moved on to pick Vesta's pockets. Soon her cape bulged with stolen gum.

Effie took her haul of gum to the van that Vesta shared with Blanche.

'Those two are bound to hang around

Pop Topper for a while,' she said to the fetch. 'They're worse show-offs than I am!'

The van was locked, but Effie crawled in through the window. Inside the van were two beds, a small table, and lots of photos of Vesta and Blanche. One of the beds had a huge pink pillow on top, with a giant 'V' stitched onto it.

'That must be Vesta's bed,' said Effie. She danced over to the bed and sat down. 'Let's get cracking,' she said, spreading packets of gum on the quilt.

The polly-fae ripped open a packet with its beak, and tipped it upside down. Round red lumps of bubblegum fell out. Effie popped one in her mouth and began to chew.

'Be careful,' said the polly-fae. 'Human junk food brings fairies out in spots!'

'I'm not *eating* this. I'm *using* it for my bad deed,' Effie said. She blew a shiny red bubble, then spat the bubblegum out into her hand.

'Open all these packets,' she said to the fetch. She stuffed more lumps into her mouth, chewed them, and spat them out. Her cheeks bulged as she chewed. The gum tasted sweet and horrible, but Effie didn't care. She was going to ruin the show, give the performance of her life, and earn a Badge of Badness all at once!

Then she rolled the chewed gum into small balls. 'Get some horsehair, Pol,' she ordered.

She had rolled up all the gum when the fetch returned with a long strand of horsehair.

Effie threaded the bubblegum balls onto the horsehair string. She knotted the

ends together and held up the bubblegum
necklace. 'This is especially for Blanche,'
she said.

Effie arranged the necklace on
Blanche's pillow.

'The next thing will be a *nose*,' Effie
said. She gathered up the rest of the
bubblegum and crawled back out the
window. 'I'm going to be busy tonight!'

9. A Bad Deed Begins

'Any minute now, they'll find out someone's been playing tricks,' said Effie the next evening. The circus folk were dressing for the performance, and she and the polly-fae were lurking in the shadows behind the dressing tent door-flap.

She was right. A shriek came from the tent. Out rushed Blanche in her bareback rider's costume. Her pink skirt bounced around her, and her necklaces and bracelets glittered. But something was wrong. Blanche's long, fluffy blonde hair wasn't flowing around her shoulders as usual. It was matted up with something red and sticky.

'Zena!' wailed Blanche, tugging at her sticky hair. 'Help! An adoring fan left me a necklace on my pillow, but now it's stuck to my hair! I put it on especially for the television camera, and it's melted all over me!'

Zena came out of her van and put her arm round the bareback rider. 'Poor Blanche! What a pity you've spoiled your looks,' she cooed. She sounded as if she cared, but Effie saw her hiding a smile.

'Help me wash it out, quickly!' yelled Blanche.

Effie giggled. 'It serves you right for calling me an outsider and ignoring my performance,' she said. Of course, Blanche didn't hear Effie through her DNM spell.

Vesta came out of the tent and joined the others. 'Blanche, why have you put bubblegum in your hair?' she said.

Blanche turned on her. 'I didn't *put* it there, you stupid child. Someone played a horrible trick on me.' She clutched at her hair again.

'We'll have to cut your hair off,'
said Zena.

Then came a yell from inside the tent.
It was Dodley.

'Now what?' asked Zena as the clown
rushed out towards them.

'By doze!' mumbled Dodley. He had
both hands over his face.

'Your nose? What's wrong with it?'
asked Zena.

'Id's duck do by vaze.'

Zena pulled Dodley's hands away,
revealing a huge, round, red clown-nose.

Effie hugged herself. Her gum fun was
working beautifully. 'Do you think he
nose what's happening to him?' she asked
the polly-fae.

Zena grabbed the nose and tugged.
'It's made out of bubblegum, just like
Blanche's necklace,' she said.

'Take it off, Dodley,' said Vesta.
'You look stupid. Pop Topper told us
to *chew* gum during the performance,
not wear it.'

'Id's duck do by vaze,' groaned Dodley,
again. 'I god do dell Barigold.'

'She won't be interested,' said Effie.

Just then, a roar came from Marigold's
van. 'Oh, yuck, what's this in my best
boots?'

*

Pop Topper couldn't wait for the show to
begin. He wanted to see his Big Pop
Gum get the attention it deserved. He
imagined the cheers from the crowd:
*Yay for Pop Topper!' 'Big Pop Gum is fun!'
'Big Pop Gum is even more exciting than the
Big Top Circus!'*

He sat down in the best seat. The
wooden benches wobbled as spectators

flocked into the big top. The smell of sawdust and popcorn drifted in the warm air, and bunches of balloons bobbed at the ends of the rows of seats.

The musicians picked up their instruments and began to play.

The television cameras began to record.

More music played. Pop Topper looked at his watch. No one had appeared in the ring. When would the show begin?

Out of the corner of his eye, he saw the trapeze sway a little, almost as if someone was swinging it. He looked up, but saw no one.

'I must be imagining things,' he muttered.

When he looked down again, a small girl in a frilly frock had appeared in the seat beside him. She seemed to have a parrot on her shoulder, but he couldn't see it very well.

'The show should have started by now,' Pop Topper said.

Effie giggled. She had cast a Glamour to change her appearance.* Pop Topper had no idea she was the same person he had seen at supper last night. 'Maybe things got a bit sticky,' she said.

'You're in for a treat,' said Pop Topper. 'Little Vesta Fiesta will do a fly-and-flip tonight. She's just a kid—about your size.'

Effie hugged herself. 'I can't wait!'

At last, Marigold limped into the spotlight, looking as though her boots didn't fit her properly. Her usually

---

*A Glamour is a magic spell which makes humans see things that are not there.

cheerful face was red and worried.

Crack! went the whip. 'Ladies and gentlemen! Welcome to the Big Top Circus!' Marigold said, shuffling her feet. 'Our first act is Ballerina Blanche Babiole and her perfect pony, *Hoopla!*'

Crack! went the whip again, and a girl ran into the ring with her pony trotting after her.

Pop Topper stared. Was that girl really Blanche Babiole? She had blonde hair, but it was short and chopped-looking as if it had been cut with a blunt pair of scissors. She wore no jewellery and her face was sulky and tear-stained.

Crack!

The girl jumped onto the pony's back. The audience yawned.

Effie turned to Pop Hooper. 'Blanche seems a bit stuck-up,' she said.

10. Dah-Dum!

Blanche's act ended, but only a few
people in the crowd clapped. Dodley
juggled, but he kept patting his pockets
and dropping his eggs.

'What's wrong with the clown?' said a
boy behind Effie. 'His nose is lumpy.'

'Yuck,' said someone else.

Dodley heard the comments, and his
face turned purple with anger. He went

on juggling, but one of the eggs flew in the wrong direction and smashed over Marigold's hat.

The audience laughed at that, but, again, hardly anyone clapped.

'This is a lovely bad deed,' said the fetch.

'Good!' said Effie. 'It's going to get better!' She watched as Zena and her tumblers cartwheeled into the ring.

The tumblers turned a few somersaults and stood upright. Then they patted their pockets, looking for packets of Big Pop Gum. But it was no use. Effie had stolen the lot.

Zena had old gum stuck to her hands and arms where she'd tried to pull off Dodley's clown nose. Soon she had sawdust stuck all over her, too.

'*Ewwww!* That's disgusting!' said the boy behind Effie.

'These circus folk are dirty,' said the woman next to him.

Marigold signalled for Zena to leave the ring.

Crack!

'Please welcome high-wire artiste *Tiny Vesta Fiesta*!' yelled Marigold.

Vesta flung out her arms. 'Ladies and gentlemen! The feat I am about to perform needs a lot of energy,' she cried. 'So it's just as well I have my Big Pop Gum!' She reached into her pocket.

Pop Topper signalled at the television camera crew to get a close-up of Vesta.

Vesta frowned, and felt in her other pocket. Then she stamped her foot. 'Someone's stolen my gum!' she yelled. 'Some horrible person wants to spoil my chance to perform on television.'

Crack! went the whip. Marigold looked

worried. 'Come on, Vesta dearie,' she hissed. 'Get on with your act, please.'

Vesta ran to the rope ladder, and climbed up it. She danced across the high wire, turning somersaults as she went. 'Now,' she announced, 'I'm going to show you my famous *fly-and-flip*!' She sprang to the trapeze and swung backwards and forwards. The music sped up.

The audience stopped rattling sweet wrappers and craned their necks to watch Vesta Fiesta do her fly-and-flip.

The music grew louder, and then made a triumphant *dah-dum!* sound. This was supposed to signal the moment when Vesta let go of the trapeze and flew through the air in a graceful flip.

Vesta tried to let go, but something was wrong.

Dah-dum! went the music again. Vesta continued to swing.

The audience laughed, and chanted, 'Fly-and-flip! Fly-and-flip! Fly-and-flip!'

Dah-dum-dum-DUM! insisted the music.

Vesta's face went red. She tried to stamp her foot in the air. 'Stop *dumming*!' she screeched. 'I *can't* fly-and-flip! My hands are stuck to the trapeze!'

Zena climbed the ladder to get Vesta unstuck from the trapeze. By then, the audience was bored. Some people booed at the performers. Others gathered up their coats and bags and walked out. Pop Topper left his seat and signalled to the cameramen to stop filming.

Effie hugged herself. Now those snobby circus people knew what it felt like to be ignored! She jumped as something pinched her ear.

'Wake up, Effie!' said the polly-fae.

'Ouch! Why did you peck me?' Effie asked.

The fetch flapped its wings. 'Here's your chance!' it squawked. 'Vesta's not going to do any fly-and-flips now.'

'Oh!' Effie gasped and jumped up. 'You're right! I've got to do *my* act and finish my big bad deed in style! Those circus folk are going to be sorry they ignored me after this.'

11. 'We Quit!'

Effie dissolved her Glamour spell, so that she looked like herself again. Then she rushed down into the ring where Marigold was watching Zena rescue Vesta. She tapped Marigold on the arm.

Marigold ignored her. 'Get that trapeze down!' she called to Zena.

'No, leave the trapeze there,' said Effie. 'I need it for my act.'

Finally Marigold turned to face her. 'What act?' she said. She stared at Effie for a moment and then frowned. 'Look, dearie, please go away. Can't you see I've got big problems here?'

Effie didn't move.

Zena helped Vesta safely to the ground. Vesta came over, white-faced with temper. 'Someone covered my trapeze with sticky stuff on purpose, to ruin my act,' she yelled. 'I bet it was *her*.' She pointed at Effie. 'That little outsider keeps hanging about because she wants to take my place!'

Marigold turned back to Effie. 'Do you know anything about Vesta's problem?' she said.

Effie giggled. 'She certainly had the audience glued to her performance . . . Oh wait. It was *Vesta* who was glued.'

'See? She admits it!' said Vesta. 'Miss Outsider ruined my act. And I suppose she ruined the others' acts, too.'

'Of course I did,' said Effie. 'You all ignored me and called me an outsider. That wasn't fair, so I let you know how it felt. Did you enjoy it when I stopped your act? Well, I didn't enjoy it when you wouldn't let me show you mine! So there.'

'Well I never!' exclaimed Marigold.

'Now that you're listening for once,' said Effie, 'let me show you what else I can do! Just watch and you'll see how the audience loves my act.'

The polly-fae put on its DNM spell and swooped to land on Effie's shoulder. 'You missed your chance again, elf.'

Effie looked about. The polly-fae was

right. The last member of the audience had just walked out. There was nothing left but empty benches.

Marigold turned pale. 'Quick!' she yelled to the musicians. 'Run out and give everyone free tickets for tomorrow's performance.'

Pop Topper came over to Marigold. 'That's that, then,' he said. 'I've never seen such a poor show. The deal is off.'

Marigold grabbed his arm. 'The next show will be perfect, I promise,' she said. 'Please give us another chance!'

'Well ... all right,' said Pop Topper. 'But only because I have already spent a lot of money on the signs. There'd better be no more problems.'

Marigold turned to Effie. 'What are we going to do with you, dearie?' she said. 'This mess is your fault.'

'Let me show you my act,' said Effie.
'You'll love it.'

'Oh, all right!' said Marigold.

'No!' yelled Vesta.

'Hush,' said Marigold. 'Let's get this
over with.' She waved to the other acts.
'Come on, everyone, take your seats.
We're going to watch the little girl's act.'

Effie clicked her heels together with

joy. 'My plan worked!' she said to the polly-fae. 'Now they know how it feels to be ignored, and Marigold is giving me a chance to show them all what an amazing performer I am!'

The polly-fae perched on a ringside seat to watch Effie's performance.

Pop Topper nodded to Effie. 'Go on then, kid. Show us your tricks.'

Effie looked about. 'Music?' she asked.

'No music,' said Marigold. 'The musicians are all giving out free tickets.'

'I'll make my own,' said Effie.

She turned to the polly-fae. 'Hide in the shadows and start squawking so the humans can hear you!' she whispered.

'OK,' said the polly-fae. It flew off behind the stands, took off its DNM spell, and began to call, *'Waaaarrrrk!'* over and over again.

Effie cast a quick Glamour to make the humans think the squawking sound they heard was lively music. Then she leapt forward in a handspring and turned somersaults around the ring.

Next, she juggled with Dodley's eggs, and then ran up the ladder to the high wire. She pranced across it, twirling on her toes, then dived towards the trapeze and flew through the air. At the top of the swing, she let go, and looped the loop, zooming down to land on Hoopla's back.

Then, she cantered around the ring, poised on one toe. At last, she bowed, bounced once and landed at Marigold's feet. 'Tah–*dah*!' she sang as her music Glamour faded. 'Did you like my act?'

The polly-fae put its DNM spell back on. 'Way to go, Effie Redwood!' it yelled.

'Top act, kid!' said Pop Topper.

They were the only ones who cheered.

Dodley, Zena, Vesta and Blanche and the others glared at Effie. Marigold stared with her mouth wide open.

'You see?' said Effie.

'You're extraordinary!' gasped Marigold.

'The kid's a star!' said Pop Topper. He turned to Marigold. 'Sign her up. She's perfect for advertising my gum.'

'You're right!' said Marigold.

'No!' yelled Vesta. 'You can't have her. She's an outsider. *I'm* the star of this circus.'

'Who wants another little show-off?' snapped Zena. 'One's enough.' She glared at Vesta.

'How dare she use my pony without permission!' said Blanche.

'Are you going to let her push in here, play horrible tricks on us, and then steal our jobs?' said Dodley.

'All I stole was a bit of bubblegum,' said Effie. 'I just wanted you to let me show you what I can do.' She beamed at Pop Topper. 'The audience will love me.'

'If you hire her, I'll quit!' said Vesta.

'I'll quit, too,' said Dodley.

Blanche held up her hands. 'We'll *all* quit if you hire her, Marigold. You can't be so unfair to us! We won't allow it.'

They folded their arms and lifted their chins.

'We *mean* it,' said Dodley.

Marigold glanced at Pop Topper.

'The kid's got what it takes,' he said. 'She's special.'

Marigold folded her arms and lifted *her* chin. 'You're right,' she said. 'We've always wanted to be the best circus in the country. To be the best, we have to hire the best acts.' She turned to Effie. 'You're hired.'

'We quit!' said Vesta.

'Nonsense,' said Marigold.

All the acts turned their backs on Marigold and left the big top.

'They can't leave now,' Effie told Marigold. 'They'll be back.'

12. 'SHOW CANCELLED!'

Effie was so excited about her bad deed, she could hardly stand still. 'Tomorrow's performance is going to be wonderful, Pol,' she told the fetch. 'I wish the elves could see me do my big act. I can't wait to show those circus folk how fabulous I am, *and* get my Badge of Badness.'

'The hags will come to the show,' said the polly-fae. 'I'll invite them now.'

'Good idea,' said Effie. 'Tell them to expect the best show ever.'

The fetch tweaked her ear in farewell, and then flew off towards the Abademy.

Effie went to the tent where the horses slept and made herself a snug nest in the hay. She put on her DNM spell. Then she curled up to sleep.

She woke with a start. Torchlight flitted through the tent, and Effie sat up to see what was happening. Blinking, she saw Blanche creeping past with a torch.

Blanche crept up to Hoopla, and untied him. 'Come on, Hoopla,' she said. 'We're quitting. Marigold can have her horrible new act if she must, but that kid will *not* be riding you.' She led the pony away.

'That's mean!' Effie said to herself. 'Now she's trying to spoil *my* act. Oh well, I can still do the other things.'

She went back to sleep.

The next time Effie woke, it was daylight. Someone was yelling outside the tent. Effie leapt up and ran out to see what was going on. She found Marigold standing with Zena just inside the big top. Zena was wearing a skirt and high-heeled shoes instead of her usual leotard. A suitcase sat beside her.

'Where is everyone?' Marigold yelled. 'It's time for rehearsal.'

'They've gone,' said Zena.

'Gone? Gone where?'

'They quit,' said Zena. 'Remember?'

'Nonsense,' said Marigold. 'Vesta's always saying she'll quit. She doesn't mean it.'

'She meant it this time,' said Zena.

'She'll be back,' said Marigold. 'In the meantime, you can do an extra turn at

the next performance. Tell the musicians
to rehearse another piece.'

Zena shook her head. 'Marigold, you
just don't get it, do you? Miss Outsider
ruined our acts and you hired her anyway.
We're leaving. The musicians have already
left. They're upset that you let Miss
Outsider use that strange recorded music
that sounded like birdsong.'

'What about the show?' yelled
Marigold.

Zena shrugged. 'Who cares?'

'But I promised Pop Topper!'

'That's not my problem,' said Zena.

Marigold looked around the empty big top. She sat down in the sawdust. 'I'm ruined,' she said. 'The Big Top Circus is finished.'

Effie removed her DNM spell and stepped closer to Marigold. 'No, it's not,' she said. 'The audience will love the show.'

'You again!' said Marigold. 'There won't be a show. There will be no acts and no musicians. They've all left.'

'I'm here,' Effie said. 'My act is the best, anyway.'

'We can't have just one act! You've ruined my circus.'

'No, I haven't!' insisted Effie. 'I'm going to do my act. The crowd will love me. They'll cheer and———'

'Get this straight,' said Marigold. 'You will *not* do your act. The circus is finished.'

She found a tin of black paint and a huge piece of card. Then, in jagged letters, she painted the words:

SHOW CANCELLED!

'No!' howled Effie. 'You can't do this!'

Marigold propped the sign up outside the big top, and turned to Zena. 'I hope you're satisfied now,' she said.

Zena picked up her case and left.

'I have to do my act!' wailed Effie.

'Go *away*!' snapped Marigold. She walked off and shut herself in her van.

Effie fled to the deserted horse tent, burrowed into the straw, and sobbed. Now she would never have a chance to belong at the Abademy!

13. 'The Show Must Go On!'

The polly-fae flapped back towards the town of Appleboffin. It wasn't wearing its DNM spell, but from that height it looked like an ordinary bird to most humans. The polly-fae was looking forward to seeing Effie Redwood win her Badge of Badness. By now, the audience should be arriving for the show.

As the polly-fae zoomed towards the

big top, it noticed that the circus seemed unnaturally quiet. A few people were even walking *away* from the big top, which was strange, because it was almost show time. Where was everyone?

The fetch found Effie crouched in the empty horses' tent. She lifted a tearful face and sniffed.

'What's going on?' asked the polly-fae. 'Where are the others? Why aren't you ready for your act?'

'There isn't going to be any act,' said Effie. 'Marigold cancelled the show. She put up a sign.' She scrubbed her eyes with her cape, then wailed, 'I never meant for the others to leave, Pol!'

The fetch stared at her with beady eyes. 'You've done a very bad deed. It's not easy for one elf to close down a whole circus.'

'But spoiling *their* acts was only part of my bad deed,' Effie said. 'For the next part, the circus folk were supposed to see the crowd cheering me and feel really envious. I'm sure *half* a bad deed isn't enough to win a Badge of Badness.' A tear ran down her cheek and dripped off her chin. 'I might as well give up and go back to the forest.'

The polly-fae glared at her. 'I'm disappointed in you, Effie Redwood,' it said. 'Think how the hags will feel! They're not young, you know. Maggie Nabbie must be almost two hundred and seventy. They're coming all this way to see a grand performance.'

Effie picked at bits of straw. 'Um . . . Will the hags *really* be disappointed?'

'They had great hopes for you,' said

the polly-fae. 'They love a good show.'

'*They* are the only ones who really want me,' said Effie. 'Except for you, Pol. Even if I can't win my Badge of Badness, I wish I could show the hags an exciting act, as a thank you.'

'Do it then!' said the fetch. 'Get rid of that sign and put on a show!'

Effie sniffled and wiped her eyes. 'All right, I will!' she said. She got up and ran to the big top.

The circus ring seemed lonely without the performers and the audience. Effie pulled the lid off the paint pot and changed the sign. Now it said:

SHOW UN-CANCELLED!

'That's better,' said the polly-fae. It flew to the lighting box and flicked on the switch.

'Please would you start squawking again?' Effie said.

'With pleasure,' said the fetch. It started to screech out a tune.

Effie cast another music Glamour, and soon cheerful tunes filled the air, and began pouring towards the town. The lights flashed and gleamed in time with the music. The big top had never looked and sounded so exciting.

When the people of Appleboffin heard
the music, they remembered that they
had free tickets for that night's show.
At first people came in a trickle, but more
and more followed, until the big top was
packed.

Pop Topper had been about to go back
to the city, but when he heard the music,
he changed his mind. He fought his way
back through the crowds and took his
seat in the front row.

It was so crowded inside the big top
that no one noticed when three tall hags
dressed in faded tartan tatters marched in
and settled beside Pop Topper.

'Evening, laddie,' said Maggie Nabbie.
'Looking forward to the show?'

Pop Topper tapped his foot. 'I'm just
pleased there's a show at all!' he said.
'I was worried it was cancelled.'

The music grew louder, and Effie bounced into the ring.

'Welcome to the Big Top Circus!' she yelled. 'My name is Effie Redwood! I don't fit in with the forest elves. The circus people didn't want me. Half a bad deed won't win me a Badge of Badness, but there is one thing I *can* do! I can put on an outrageous show!' She did backflips around the ring, and then leapt high in the air. 'Tah-*dah*!'

The audience applauded, but Effie was on the move again, whirling over and over, turning cartwheels. Then she juggled with eggs and rushed up the ladder to dance on the high wire.

'*Wheeeee!*' she cried, swooping on the flying trapeze.

'Yay! Way to go, Effie Redwood!' squawked the polly-fae.

Effie let go of the trapeze and looped the loop twice before she bounced into the safety net. She bounced so high, she caught the bar of the trapeze again.

The audience gasped and applauded, and Effie laughed. She might have failed in her big bad deed, but she could still entertain the hags.

'Now *this*,' she cried, 'is what I call my famous flying flip!'

14. 'Show Time!'

As Zena walked to Appleboffin train station, she thought she saw a strange red-eyed parrot flying overhead in the direction of the Big Top Circus.

'There are no wild parrots around here,' she muttered. 'I must be seeing things.'

She found Vesta, Dodley, Blanche and Hoopla waiting for the next train to a nearby city.

'The show's cancelled,' Zena said. 'The circus is done for.'

Vesta sniffed. 'It serves Auntie Marigold right. She was so sure we wouldn't leave.'

'She shouldn't have let that horrible little girl join,' said Dodley.

'She was just a nasty show-off,' agreed Vesta.

'I wish I'd left before,' said Blanche. 'Then I'd still have my beautiful hair.'

The performers sighed and fell silent.

They were still sulking when Hoopla raised his head and neighed.

'He knows it should be show time,' said Blanche. 'He thinks he hears circus music.'

Zena looked up. 'He *can* hear circus music,' she said. 'Listen.'

The artistes exchanged glances. 'It can't be from the circus,' said Dodley. 'The musicians caught the first train out of Appleboffin this morning.'

Blanche jumped onto Hoopla's back. 'Let's go and see,' she said. 'We can always catch a later train.' She cantered off.

The other acts looked at one another, and ran after her.

*

Marigold woke as the music began. She lay on her bunk for a long time, wondering what was going on. Finally, she decided she must be imagining things, and was trying to get back to sleep when she heard hoofbeats outside her van. She tumbled off the bunk, hurried outside, and spotted Blanche riding up on Hoopla.

'Blanche!' she cried. 'You're back!'

Then she looked down the street and saw the other circus acts running towards her. 'Here come the others!'

'We're not here to perform,' said Blanche, pulling up. 'We just want to know what's going on.' She walked Hoopla into the big top where Effie was showing off her flying flip. The other artistes arrived, hot and out of breath. They piled in behind Blanche.

Effie swooped from the trapeze and bounced back into the safety net. Then she sprang onto Dodley's trampoline and bounced into a triple loop the loop.

The audience yelled with delight.

'They never cheer for us like that,' complained Blanche.

'They'll cheer for me!' snapped Dodley, pulling on his costume.

'Go on then,' said Blanche. 'Show us.'

Dodley rushed into the ring, and jumped onto the trampoline, just as Effie landed on its springy surface.

She was about to tell Dodley to get out of the way when she had an idea.

'*Wheeeeee!*' she yelled. 'Dodley, you're about to give the best show of your life!' She grabbed his hands and bounced high.

Dodley found himself flying towards the ceiling in a perfect triple somersault. The audience applauded wildly as the elf and the clown tumbled through the air. Up and over they went, again and again. Eventually they bounced right up and sat on the bar of the trapeze.

Dodley couldn't believe it.

Neither could Marigold. 'Ladies and gentlemen!' she roared. 'I give you Effie Redwood and Dodley the *Flying Clown*!'

The audience cheered.

Zena cartwheeled into the ring, high-heeled shoes and all. 'I'm not going to be left out of this!' she yelled.

Effie left Dodley swinging from the trapeze and swooped into a backflip. 'An elf flies! The humans follow! They fly today, but not tomorrow!' she sang.

Then Vesta, Blanche and all the other performers ran into the ring. They followed Effie in turning a somersault. In seconds the ring was full of flying, tumbling, laughing humans and one outrageous elf.

Above them all flew the polly-fae, cheering at the top of its voice. 'Way to go, Effie! Hurrah for Effie Redwood!'

15. Badge of Badness

After the show, the circus folk were very pleased with themselves.

'Did you enjoy my act?' asked Effie.

'I was *wonderful*,' said Dodley. 'I was at the top of my game!'

'I flew-and-flipped twice as far!' burst in Vesta. 'Auntie Marigold will have to give me extra-top billing now.'

'But did you enjoy *my* act?' asked Effie.

'It was all right,' said Blanche, 'but did you see the triple spin I did on Hoopla? The crowd went wild! I can't wait until tomorrow when we can do it all again!'

'It'll be a whole new show,' gloated Zena.

'So it will,' said Effie, and smiled. 'It will be a very different show tomorrow. It's a pity I won't be here to see it.'

'But you have to stay with us now,' said Zena.

'Yes,' said Dodley. 'You must help me perfect that trampoline act.'

'I'm sure Auntie Marigold will find a place for you, if I ask her nicely,' said Vesta.

'No, thanks,' said Effie. 'I have a better place to go.' She turned and walked away.

'Effie! Effie! Please come back!' called the circus folk. 'We need you!

You belong here! Pop Topper might cancel his deal if you quit!'

Effie didn't even look back.

The polly-fae swooped onto her shoulder. 'The hags want to see you,' it said.

Effie followed the fetch's directions to the back of the circus ground. There, she found three tall hags perched on the back of a truck.

'So you're the lassie who wants a Badge of Badness,' said Maggie Nabbie.

'Yes,' said Effie. 'My first bad deed turned out all wrong. So then I helped those snobby circus folk give the best performances of their lives!'

'And *that's* your bad deed?' said Maggie Nabbie.

'Yes, it is,' said Effie. 'They are so pleased with themselves, they can't wait to do it all again tomorrow. But guess what? They won't be able to do it tomorrow, *or ever again*, because I won't be here to help them. They'll be furious.'

There was a silence. Effie held her breath. She had done her very worst, but was it bad enough for a place at the Abademy?

'Aye, that's a deed that deserves a Badge of Badness,' said Maggie Nabbie.

She reached inside her tartan tatters and
pulled out a shining red badge. The
polly-fae squawked with delight and
looped the loop. The hags applauded,
and a skirl of bagpipes echoed around the
circus lot.

Effie took the badge. It looked like a
lump of red bubblegum.

Effie pinned the badge to her chest.
'I think I'm going to fit right in at this
Abademy!' she said.

A Note from Tiffany Mandrake

Psst, this is me, Tiffany Mandrake, again.

Effie still shows off, but that's fine, because the hags and the other Little Horrors love to watch her performance at the Abademy of Badness. Oh, and so do I! We all get together and yell with the polly-fae: 'Way to go, Effie Redwood!'

The Big Top Circus did lose its deal with Pop Topper, but some good came out of Effie's visit after all. Marigold's acts work extremely hard to be the best they can be, so everyone loves the show. And sometimes they think of the night they gave the performances of their lives.

I live in a cosy, creepy cottage in the Abademy grounds. The hags know I'm here, and they trust me completely.

They know I'll never say a word . . . and I haven't . . .

. . . except to you.

About the Author

Bad behaviour is nothing new to Tiffany Mandrake—some of her best friends are Little Horrors! And all sorts of magical visitors come to her cosy, creepy cottage in the grounds of the Hags' Abademy.

Tiffany's favourite creature is the dragon who lives in her cupboard and heats water for her bath. She rather hopes the skunk-fae doesn't come to visit again, for obvious reasons.

About the Artist

Martin Chatterton once had a dog called Sam, who looked exactly like a cocker spaniel ... except she was much smaller and had wings. According to Martin, she even used to flutter around his head and say annoying things. Hmmm!

Martin has done so many bad deeds he is sure he deserves several Badges of Badness. 'Never trust a good person' is his motto.